Copyright © 2019 Clavis Publishing Inc., New York

Originally published as *Ridder Tim is een beetje jaloers* in Belgium and the Netherlands by Clavis Uitgeverij, 2018
English translation from the Dutch by Clavis Publishing Inc., New York

Visit us on the Web at www.clavis-publishing.com.

No part of this publication may be reproduced or stored in a retrieval system,
or transmitted in any form or by any means, electronic, mechanical, photocopying,
recording, or otherwise, without the prior written permission of the publisher,
except in the case of brief quotations embodied in critical articles and reviews.
For information regarding permissions, write to Clavis Publishing, info-US@clavisbooks.com.

Sir Tim Is a Little Jealous written by Judith Koppens and illustrated by Eline van Lindenhuizen

ISBN 978-1-60537-492-5 (hardcover edition)
ISBN 978-1-60537-502-1 (softcover edition)

This book was printed in August 2019 at Nikara, M. R. Štefánika 858/25, 963 01 Krupina, Slovakia.

First Edition
10 9 8 7 6 5 4 3 2 1

Sir Tim
Is a Little Jealous

Written by Judith Koppens
Illustrated by Eline van Lindenhuizen

Clavis

NEW YORK

It's a beautiful day. Sir Tim is going to the playground with his friend Sara.

"Come on, Dragon," Tim calls to his dog.

"We're almost there."

Dragon wags his tail. "Hey, look!" Sara points.

"There's Max. Let's go and play with him!"

And before Tim can say anything, she's gone.

"Hi, Sara," calls Max cheerfully. "Let's go play on the swing!
I'll give you a push." Max and Sara run to the swing, but Tim doesn't run along.
He doesn't feel like playing on the swing and he also has a strange feeling in his tummy.

Max and Sara cheer. "Higher, Max!" calls Sara.

"High as the birds in the sky!" Max pushes Sara as hard as he can.

Tim watches from the log. Now his belly hurts a little more.

Doesn't Sara like him anymore?

Tim has an idea.

"Watch this, Dragon," says Tim.

"If I climb to the top, Sara will think I'm brave."

"Look, Sara!" Tim yells.

"Look at me! Look how brave I am!" Sara can't hear Tim.

She's too busy pushing Max on the swing.

"Maybe Sara will notice me if I walk on the balance beam," Tim says to Dragon.

"Look, Sara!" calls Tim proudly.

"Look at me! Look how fast I go!" Sara waves at Tim.

She's on the seesaw with Max. Every time when Max hits the ground,

Sara jumps a bit. "Woo-hoo!" she laughs.

"Come on, Dragon," says Tim. "We'll go to the ropes.
If I swing on this rope, Sara will think I'm very strong."
He grabs a rope and begins to climb.
"Look, Sara!" calls Tim.
"Look at me! Look how strong I am!" Sara doesn't see Tim.
She's still too busy laughing and playing with Max.

"I don't know what to do next, Dragon," sighs Tim.

"Sara doesn't even notice me. She's only playing with Max."

Dragon gives Sir Tim a comforting lick on his face.

Tim looks up and thinks. "Wait a sec . . ." he suddenly says.

"If I swing like a monkey, maybe Sara will think I am funny.

Then she'll laugh with me, too."

Sir Tim climbs up the tree and swings on a high branch.

"Look, Sara!" calls Tim. "Look at me! Look what I'm doing!"

He hangs from the branch with one hand.

He scratches his armpit with the other hand.

"Oo, oo, oo!" he calls. "I'm a monkey!"

But then the branch begins to crack. Crr-crr-crrack!
The branch breaks and Sir Tim falls down.
Dragon starts to bark.

Sara hears Dragon and then she
sees Tim lying on the ground.
"Tim!" she calls, frightened.
"Sir Tim, are you hurt?"

Sir Tim is a little hurt, but he likes that Sara's there.

"I thought you didn't like me anymore," he whispers.

"You were only playing with Max."

"Silly Tim." Sara laughs. "I think you're a bit jealous."

Tim starts to blush.

"I sometimes play with other kids,

but that doesn't mean that I don't like you anymore."

"Next time we come to the playground, we can all play together,"
Sara adds.

Tim gives her a questioning look.

"You don't have to worry," she says with a smile.

"You will always be my best friend."